BUDDY & HIS BIG TRUCK

Lisa Cassman

Enjoy your
ride with Buddy!.
L Cassman

Halo
PUBLISHING
INTERNATIONAL

ISBN: 978-1-63765-001-1
LCCN: 2021905216

Halo Publishing International, LLC
8000 W Interstate 10, Suite 600
San Antonio, Texas 78230
www.halopublishing.com

Printed and bound in the United States of America

I would like to dedicate this book
to my husband, Steve! Thanks for
all the truck adventures.

Also, to our grandkids,
who have a love for trucks.

What is a semi?

A semi is a big truck, with a long trailer, that hauls goods to the store.

Who drives a truck?

Maybe your dad, mom, grandpa, grandma, uncle, aunt, or cousin.

Could also be a brother, sister, or close friend.

5

Buddy is taking a drive in a big truck.

He leaves from home in the truck.

He could also be leaving from a company terminal to get the truck and trailer.

Where does Buddy get his trailer loaded with goods?

He drives to a big warehouse.

What do you think Buddy can haul in his trailer?

He can haul many goods to the store, so we can buy our groceries and other needs.

For how long do you think Buddy is away?

Sometimes he may be home every day and sometimes away for a week at a time.

He could even be away driving for a month or two.

9

What do you think Buddy sees along the way?

He may see fields with corn, hay, or even farms with cows.

He may see big cities with lots of lights.

He may see big, beautiful mountains up close or in the distance.

He drives in all types of weather.

Snow, rain, thunderstorms,
and even sunshine.

Like all truck drivers, Buddy drives
safe by watching in his mirrors
and focusing on his surroundings.

Buddy may get a short load requiring only a few hours or miles of driving.

Or maybe a longer load, where he will have to drive a day or two for many miles.

When he drives a long time, where does Buddy sleep?

He finds a truck stop or somewhere that a truck and trailer can park.

Where will Buddy eat?

He may have food with him in his truck, or he can eat at a truck stop or restaurant.

When he wants to finally sleep for the night, he has a bed in his truck, called a "bunk," to sleep in.

Buddy's family misses
him when he is gone.

And he misses them.

How can Buddy keep in
touch with his family?

He has a phone or tablet he
can call or video-chat on.

After a good night's sleep, Buddy finally reaches his destination.

To be unloaded, he backs the trailer into the big doors.

When the trailer is empty, Buddy then may get another load to take somewhere else, or he drives home for a short break.

21

While on the road, Buddy can talk with other drivers.

He talks to them on a CB radio.

This is the life of a real trucker.

That's a big 10-4.

Safe travels, drivers!

This is Buddy signing off for now.

Catch you on the flip-flop.

CPSIA information can be obtained
at www.ICGtesting.com
Printed in the USA
BVHW020343260421
605091BV00002B/2

9 781637 650011